A Cunning Plan

and

The Holiday Nobody Wanted

Contents

A Cunning Plan

By Sally Cowan

Illustrated by Tom Jellett

Characters

Narrator

Monica
11 years old

Rachel
Monica's younger sister

Julia
Monica and Rachel's mum

Rob
Monica and Rachel's dad

Max
Monica and Rachel's cousin

Gus
Max's younger brother

Karen
Max and Gus's mum

Dimitri
Max and Gus's dad

Harry
Gus's friend

Narrator

It was the weekend, and Monica and Rachel were at home playing board games with their cousins, Max and Gus. They were all due at the boys' place for lunch.

Max was annoyed because the girls had won every game so far.

Max

Come on, let's stop playing board games! My parents will be expecting us soon. Let's have a race to our place.

Monica

Max, you're the school sprinting champ. What chance do we have against you?

Gus

Yes, and because I'm the youngest, I'm sure to come last!

Rachel

Why don't we race in teams? Monica and I against you two boys. The first team to touch your front gate is the winner!

Monica

The losers have to do the dishes after lunch!

Max *(enthusiastically)*

Okay! You know, our dad's got cooking fever at the moment. He's always watching that TV show, *Top Chef*, and trying to make the most complicated recipes.

Rachel *(rubbing her stomach)*

Lucky you! Uncle Dimitri's a great cook!

Max *(groaning)*

Yeah, the food *is* great, but he uses *every* dish in the kitchen!

Gus *(quietly, to Max)*

But, Max, if we're in a team together, I might slow you down.

Max *(whispering to Gus)*

Don't worry, I have a plan … a cunning plan.

(to the girls)

Yes, Gus and I are definitely up for it!

Monica

I'll ask Mum and Dad to start the race, so there's no cheating.

Narrator

They all went outside. Rachel was whispering something to Monica that made them both giggle, while the boys were whispering tactics.

Julia

Okay, everyone. Take the walking track next to the beach, then up the steps, past the lighthouse and along the street to Karen and Dimitri's place.

Rob

We'll meet you there for lunch. Are you ready? On your marks, get set, GO!

Narrator

The teams raced to the end of the road, where the walking track began.

Rachel *(quietly, to Monica)*

Hey, Monica. That shortcut I told you about will be coming up soon. Let's sprint ahead so the boys don't see us take it.

Narrator

Suddenly, Gus stopped in the middle of the track, moaning. The other three slowed down to look back.

Gus *(moaning)*

Ow! I've got a stitch. Max, wait for me!

Max *(annoyed)*

What, already? Come on, Gus!

Rachel *(chuckling, to Monica)*

Hmm, I don't think we'll need to sprint. Gus is going to be hopeless.

Monica *(laughing)*

Hey, boys! We'll make sure the dishwashing gloves are ready for you! We are going to love watching you two lose – again!

Narrator

And with that, the girls headed off around a bend in the track. But Max and Gus weren't worried.

Max *(giving Gus a high five)*

Nicely done, Gus. You fooled them completely. Okay, stay here. I'll be back soon. We'll show those girls they can't always win!

Narrator

Max sprinted back to his cousins' house. He grabbed Monica's bike, which he'd noticed earlier was leaning against the shed. He rode back along the track to find Gus. In the meantime, the girls had come to a break in the bushes, next to the track.

Rachel

Here's the shortcut. It will take about ten minutes off our run.

Monica *(doubtfully)*

Are you sure this is it? The bush looks awfully thick in there.

Rachel

Yes, this is it. See how the lighthouse is straight ahead? We just need to head towards it. We'll come out near the bottom of the steps; then run up past the lighthouse to Max and Gus's gate – well before them!

Narrator

Back on the track, Max had quickly caught up to Gus. Their plan was for Gus to ride Monica's bike, while Max ran next to him. That way, Gus would be able to keep up. But they would have to take a different, slightly longer, route so that the girls didn't see Gus riding the bike.

Gus *(excitedly)*

This is a great plan, Max!

Max

Yeah, those girls think they are so good. Imagine the looks on their faces when they see us relaxing at home, waiting for them!

Narrator

Meanwhile, somewhere in the bushes …

Rachel

(miming pushing past branches)

This bush is a lot thicker than I remember it. But … I haven't used this shortcut for quite a while.

Monica *(annoyed)*

Obviously nobody else has either! This may not have been such a good idea, Rachel. *Ouch!* What's that? Help, I can't move, something's got me!

Rachel

Don't worry! It's just a branch – your shirt is caught. Keep still while I untangle it.

Narrator

At the same time, Max and Gus were making good progress.

Gus

We're going to win easily, Max.

Max *(puffing a little)*

Yes … we should … get to the front gate … well before the girls.

Narrator

The boys had taken the longer track and were already at the bottom of the steps near the lighthouse.

Max

Come on, Gus! Let's run up. We're almost home.

Gus

But what'll we do with Monica's bike? The girls will see it if we leave it here.

Narrator

Just then, Gus's friend, Harry, came walking out of his house. Harry lived in the street at the foot of the lighthouse cliff.

Harry

Hi, Gus! Do you want to come to my place?

Hey, what are you doing with that girls' bike?

Gus

It's our cousin's bike – and it's a long story. I haven't got time to explain.

Max *(quickly)*

Harry, can we leave the bike at your place? We'll come back to get it later. We've got to get home now. Come on, Gus! They'll be catching up!

Harry *(excitedly)*

Oh, is this some kind of race? Sure, I'll keep the bike here. Good luck – I hope you win!

Narrator

In the meantime, the girls were clambering out of the bushes. Bits of twig and leaves were stuck in their hair and caught on their clothes.

Monica *(hopefully)*

Surely we're nearly at the steps, Rachel!

Rachel

We just have to go along the edge of the wetlands. Be careful! This ground is soaking wet.

Monica *(sighing)*

Look at my shoes. They're covered in mud!

Narrator

The girls sloshed along next to the wetlands and then ran for the steps, just in time to see Max and Gus climbing up ahead of them.

Monica *(to Rachel, grumpily)*

How did *they* get here before us? So much for your shortcut, Rachel!

Rachel *(looking puzzled)*

I thought for sure that we would be first!

Narrator

Monica and Rachel's mum and dad had driven to Dimitri and Karen's place. They were all waiting in the front yard.

Julia

Here they come!

Dimitri

It's going to be close!

Narrator

The cousins all raced towards the front gate, but Max and Gus reached it first.

Max *(laughing)*

Yes! We won!

Karen *(proudly)*

Well done, boys! Wow, Gus, how did you keep up with Max? You're hardly puffing at all!

Rachel *(puffing)*

It's not possible, Auntie Karen – we were way ahead, and Gus had a stitch!

Julia *(surprised)*

Girls, what happened to you?

Rob

How did you get so dirty?

Narrator

Just then, Harry arrived. He had followed everyone up the steps and saw Max and Gus celebrating their victory.

Harry *(pleased)*

Hey, Gus and Max, you won! Do you want to play tennis later? We can go when you come back to pick up the bike.

Monica *(suspiciously)*

Bike? What bike?

Gus *(sheepishly)*

Oh, er …

Harry

The girls' bike.

(to Monica)

Oh, is it yours?

Rachel *(gleefully, folding her arms)*

Ah, ha! That's how they made it so fast! I knew they must have cheated!

Monica

Well, I guess we all cheated. Rachel and I took a shortcut through the bush.

Max

I was wondering how *you* got here so fast!

Monica

Looks like we'll *all* be doing the dishes after lunch!

Dimitri

The dishes? What dishes? We're having a sausage sizzle.

Karen

And I thought we'd go out for an ice cream later.

Monica *(happily)*

You know what that means, everyone?

Max, Rachel and Gus

Yes! No dirty dishes!

The Holiday Nobody Wanted

By Sally Cowan and Debbie Croft

Illustrated by Tom Jellett

Characters:

Narrator

Monica
11 years old

Rachel
Monica's younger sister

Julia
Monica and Rachel's mum

Rob
Monica and Rachel's dad

Max
Monica and Rachel's cousin

Gus
Max's younger brother

Karen
Max and Gus's mum

Dimitri
Max and Gus's dad

Narrator

Max and Gus, and their cousins, Monica and Rachel, ran along the beach. Gus flopped down on the sand and the others joined him, pleased to have the chance for a rest.

Rachel

What is your family doing for the summer holidays this year, Max?

Max

Who knows? Mum and Dad wouldn't even have had time to think about that yet. They work so hard, holiday plans always seem to get left until the last minute.

What about your family? Where are you going?

Monica

Hmm, I don't think our parents have made any plans either, have they, Rachel?

Rachel

No, at least, not that I've heard of. Maybe we should talk to them about it.

Gus

Maybe we should do that, too, Max.

Monica

I'd give anything to go ice-skating! It doesn't look too difficult.

Rachel

Well, I certainly don't want to be heading off to a cold climate where all we do is get wet and shiver from the ice and snow. I'm hoping we can all go to Brookville to see "The Wonder Jets" in concert. That would be fantastic!

Max

Hmmm. I just need to be where there is reliable internet access. I'm in an online chess tournament, and I don't want to let the other team members down by not being available.

Monica

What about you, Gus? Where would you like to go for the holidays?

Gus

Well, there's this fabulous new horse ranch up in the mountains. I know I can't have a horse while we live here, but I'd like to learn to ride properly.

Narrator

At the same time, the parents of the four children were sitting on the deck at Karen and Dimitri's house, and the topic of holidays was brought up.

Rob

If you haven't made any plans, maybe our two families could go somewhere together. Why don't we give it some thought and allow the children to help us decide where to go?

Julia

They would love that!

Karen

I honestly haven't given the holidays any thought yet, but that sounds like a great idea! For years, I've wanted to go rock climbing, so I'd like to fit that in.

Dimitri

I've heard there are some Mexican cooking demonstrations on in the city, where they teach people how to use a huge selection of mouth-tingling spices. Maybe then I could create a whole new range of dishes! Oohhh ... my tastebuds are "Dimitricing" just thinking about it!

Karen

That's a great idea, Dimitri. It's always wonderful when you venture into a new area of cooking! Your recipes are always so ... different.

(speaking to Julia and Rob)

What would you like to do?

Rob

Well, I've just joined the birdwatching club and I want to find some rare and exotic birds – something like the red-throated, bush-hopping wren!

Julia

It's a great idea to sort out our holidays, but I don't want to be trapped in a tent while you're off birdwatching. A holiday is for everyone, so we all need to be able to do the things we like.

Rob

That seems fair – so what would you like to do?

Julia

I have my new camera, so I'd like to take some fascinating photographs … scenery, buildings, people, you know, things like that. But I'd like to stay somewhere a little more elegant than a camping site!

Dimitri

I think we should gather the children together and let them consider the options. After all, it's their holiday, too.

Rob

I agree! Let's all meet at our house at seven o'clock tonight. We can have our plans finalised before bedtime!

Narrator

And so, a little before 7 pm, all eight people met at Julia and Rob's house. The children were very excited at the idea of being invited to help plan their annual holidays.

One by one, the adults told the children their ideas, each trying to make their suggestion sound better than all the others.

The children looked at each other and grimaced. This wasn't at all what they had in mind!

Rob

So, there you are – such a wide range of choices. Don't be influenced by what others think, just choose one activity and write it down on a piece of paper. Then the activity with the most votes, wins!

Narrator

Julia handed out eight pencils and pieces of paper. After each person had recorded their decision, Dimitri collected the folded pieces of paper and put them in a dish.

Monica

Gus, you read them out one by one and Max, you can keep the score.

Gus

The first vote is for Brookville, to see "The Wonder Jets" perform.

Karen

Now that's certainly different!

Gus

And the next vote is for … horse riding.

Julia

Horse riding? I wonder who wanted that?

Gus

The third vote goes to “anywhere that has internet access”.

Dimitri

What? That's really strange …

Gus

Number 4 says "location ideal for ice-skating".

Rob

Ice-skating? Wow! That would be "cool"!

Monica

Oh, Dad! That's such a bad Dad Joke!

Narrator

As Gus read out the remaining votes, it was clear that all the adults voted for the activity they had described a few moments earlier.

So, what's the result, Max?

Max

Well … umm … er … I'm not sure. We actually have eight possible places to go for our holidays!

Monica

But, wait a minute. I think we don't need to go anywhere for our holiday. Everything we need is right here.

Narrator

Rob looked at Monica with a puzzled expression.

Monica

Well, Max can certainly stay here and play in the chess competition.

Julia

And I was speaking with Harry's mum today and Harry is getting a horse for his birthday. She said Gus can visit any time he likes to learn to ride.

Rob

I suppose I could go over by the wetlands and do some birdwatching. There are sure to be lots of interesting two-legged creatures there.

Karen

I saw a fabulous new cookbook when I was at the shops last week. It was called *Marvellous Mexican Mouthfuls*, and it's packed with recipes featuring all sorts of exotic spices. Sounds promising for you, Dimitri.

Rachel

And, Auntie Karen, did you realise the new indoor sports centre has a rock-climbing wall? We went there for sport last Friday. It was so much fun!

Dimitri

I saw some holiday activities advertised in today's paper. One advertisement said the local council was setting up a mobile ice-skating rink. So Monica should be pleased!

Narrator

A *beep, beep* on a mobile phone interrupted the discussion. Rachel reached into her pocket and everyone saw her face break into a wide grin!

Rachel

Brilliant! It's a text from my friend, Soukie, to let me know that "The Wonder Jets" are performing at the local Entertainment Centre and she's won two free tickets. What a coincidence!

Gus

But what will you do, Auntie Julia?

Julia

Oh, Gus, you're very thoughtful. I'm going to be sneaking around watching everyone, taking spectacular photographs of everyone doing their favourite activity!

Then, I'll invite you all to my digital slide show called … "The Holiday Nobody Wanted!"

J
WJ